THE COUNT OF MONTE CRISTO

RETOLD BY PAULINE FRANCIS

Published by Evans Brothers Limited
2A Portman Mansions
Chiltern Street
London W1U 6NR

© Evans Brothers Limited 2008
First published 2008

Printed in China

British Library Cataloguing in Publication data
Francis, Pauline
   The Count of Monte Cristo. - (Fast track classics)
   1. False imprisonment - England - Juvenile fiction
   2. Napoleonic Wars, 1800-1815 - Juvenile fiction
   3. Adventure stories 4. Children's stories
   I. Title II. Dumas, Alexandre, 1802-1870
   823.9'2[J]

ISBN: 9780237534424

VISIT OUR WEBSITE
www.evansbooks.co.uk
Evans

THE COUNT OF MONTE CRISTO

Introduction

Alexandre Dumas was born in 1802, in France. His father died when he was only four years old, and he received a poor education.

The Count of Monte Cristo was published as a newspaper serial during 1844 and 1845. It tells the story of Edmond Dantès, who is wrongly imprisoned. He manages to escape and seeks revenge on those who were responsible. This revenge is long and carefully plotted. It is a story of great adventure, enjoyed by all age groups for its complicated plot and array of characters – and for its clever use of disguise.

The beginning of the story is set against the events of 1815, when the exiled emperor of France, Napoleon Bonaparte, escaped from the island of Elba. The king of France fled and Napoleon became emperor again – for one hundred days. Napoleon was later exiled once more, and the French king was restored. Those who supported the king were called Royalists and those who supported Napoleon were called Bonapartists.

Alexandre Dumas is also well known as the author of *The Three Musketeers,* which also appeared as a newspaper serial.

Dumas built a house called the Château de Monte Cristo, which he had to sell when he was short of money. In the last years of his life, Dumas travelled widely in Europe. He died in 1870, at the age of 68, in Dieppe in northern France.

At the end of February, in 1815, Edmond Dantès was sailing into the harbour of Marseilles, in the south of France. He was almost twenty, tall and slim, with dark hair and dark eyes – and he was the happiest man alive. He was about to marry his fiancée, a beautiful Spanish girl called Mercédès.

But Dantès did not know that storm clouds were already gathering, and that his life was about to change for ever...all because the captain of his ship, who was dying of a fever, had asked Edmond to deliver a letter to the island of Elba on his way home.

CHAPTER ONE

The Plot

Following a visit to his father's house, Edmond hurried to the home of Mercédès, his fiancée. Meanwhile his shipmate, Danglars, sat drinking wine with Edmond's neighbour, Caderousse, and with a young man called Fernand, who was also in love with Mercédès.

'Let's all drink to Edmond Dantès!' Danglars cried. 'The man who will soon be the new ship's captain *and* the husband of the beautiful Mercédès!'

Fernand threw his glass to the ground at the mention of Dantès. 'Mercédès once told me that if Edmond died, she'd kill herself,' he said.

'Well, he doesn't have to *die!*' the cunning Danglars said. 'What if…what if he was just…in prison?'

Then I could be captain of the ship, he thought.

'When people get out of prison, they always want revenge,' Caderousse said. 'Anyway, I like Dantès. So let's have no more of this drunken talk!'

'You remember that Dantès delivered a letter to Napoleon, on Elba,' Danglars went on. 'What if we tell the king's prosecutor that Dantès is a Bonapartist spy…and if I disguise my handwriting…'

"We denounce Edmond Dantès," Danglars wrote. *"He carried a letter to Napoleon Bonaparte on Elba and brought back a letter from him to take to his supporters in Paris. If you arrest him, you will find this letter…"*

Then, pretending that he had written it in jest, Danglars crumpled up the letter and threw it away. Taking

Caderousse by the arm, he staggered off. But when he glanced back, he saw Fernand picking up the letter.

'Now we'll let the matter take its course,' he muttered.

The day of Dantès' marriage to Mercédès dawned fine. Neither of them noticed the strange smile on Fernand's face. As the guests gathered before the marriage ceremony, Fernand wiped large beads of sweat from his brow. Suddenly, three knocks sounded at the door and a commissioner of police came in.

'Monsieur Dantès!' he shouted. 'I arrest you in the name of the law!'

'But why?' Dantès asked, his face turning pale.

'Oh no!' Caderousse whispered to Danglars. 'Is this something to do with our joke yesterday? If so, it's a cruel one.'

'I tore up the letter,' Danglars replied.

'No you didn't!' Caderousse cried. 'You threw it on the ground!'

'Hold your tongue!' Danglars said. 'You were too drunk to see anything.'

As a carriage took Dantès away, a stunned silence fell over the guests, except for the sound of Mercédès weeping. Monsieur Morrel, the owner of the ship and Edmond's employer, followed him into Marseilles, desperate to find out what was happening. He came back with terrible news.

'Well, my friends,' he said, shaking his head. 'It is more serious than we thought. Edmond is accused of being a secret agent of Napoleon Bonaparte.'

Mercédès gave a cry. Old Dantès, Edmond's father, sank back in his chair.

'So,' Caderousse muttered. 'You lied to me, Danglars. The trick was played after all.'

***

Monsieur de Villefort was as happy as any man could be. At the age of 26, he was now the crown prosecutor's deputy in Marseilles, and was engaged to be married to a rich and well-connected girl whom he loved. He supported the French king and had no sympathy for any Bonapartists who came his way.

When Dantès entered Villefort's office, he was pale, but calm and smiling.

I've done nothing wrong, he thought.

'Tell me about yourself,' Villefort began, 'and your political views. Some say that you support Napoleon?'

'I'm ashamed to say that I have *no* political views,'
Dantès replied. 'I have three feelings: I love my father, I
respect Monsieur Morrel and I adore my fiancée Mercédès.
There's little else I can tell you.'

'Let me have the letter that was given to you on Elba,'
Villefort said. 'Then you will be free to go.'

'You must have it there with all the papers that were
taken from me,' Dantès said.

'To whom was it addressed?' Villefort asked.

'A Monsieur Noirtier, in Paris,' Dantès replied. 'Do you
know him, sir?'

The colour drained from Villefort's face. 'No!' he cried,
searching through the pile of papers on his desk. As soon as
he had found it, he read it, then threw it onto the fire. 'The
main evidence against you is that letter,' he said, 'and, as
you see, I have destroyed it. Tell nobody about this.'

Dantès, giving Villefort a look of gratitude, was led
from the office to a prison cell. That night, a carriage came
for him. Certain that Villefort had sent it to take him home,
he got in. But it took him to the quayside, where he was
escorted to a boat.

Where are they taking me? Dantès thought. *Well, I've
nothing to fear, for Villefort gave me his word.*

As they rowed, a strange shape loomed in the darkness.

'My God!' Dantès cried. 'That's the prison of Château
d'If! Only political prisoners go there! Why are they taking
me to such a terrible place?'

Nobody would answer his questions. And later, alone in
his dark and damp dungeon, Dantès sank into despair.

CHAPTER TWO

Number 34 and Number 27

As a prisoner, Dantès went through every stage of misery: pride, because he knew that he was innocent; doubt, because he might be guilty without knowing it; and hope that the guards might let him have books and exercise – or even a cell-mate. When all failed, he turned to God.

But he still remained a prisoner – number 34.

Dantès was a simple and uneducated man and had nothing to distract his mind. He cursed aloud and threw himself against the walls of his prison.

'My happiness has been destroyed for no reason that I know of,' he said to himself.

Four years passed in this way.

And, unknown to him, the note in his prison file read:

EDMOND DANTES: This prisoner played an active part in Bonaparte's escape from the island of Elba, which led to the overthrow of King Louis XVIII. To be kept in solitary confinement.

One night, Dantès heard a scratching sound on his wall, but, used to rats, he took little notice. It went on, hour after hour. At last, he picked up a stone and knocked three times on the wall. When the noise stopped, Dantès felt the hair rise on his neck.

'Who are you?' he cried.

'I am…I am Number 27,' a voice replied.

Dantès began to dig towards the sound. At last, at the bottom of a dark pit behind the wall of Dantès' cell, a white-haired man appeared. He must have been more than

60 years old. He had been a priest - Father Faria – and he had been digging for three years.

'I've never thought of trying to escape,' Dantès told him. 'I thought that even if I got outside, there's only a sheer drop to the sea from the rocks. Then I'd have to swim for my life.'

At night, when the guards were asleep, the two men talked in Faria's cell.

'Edmond, who would benefit by your disappearance?' Faria asked.

'Nobody!'

Dantès answered all Faria's questions: 'Yes, one man on the ship disliked me, Danglars...Yes, a man named Fernand was in love with Mercédès...Yes, I saw Danglars, Fernand and Caderousse drinking together...Yes, I brought a letter from Elba but the deputy prosecutor burned it…that was the only thing that could have caused trouble...it was addressed to a Monsieur Noirtier…'

'And the deputy prosecutor's name?' Faria asked.

'Monsieur de Villefort,' Dantès replied.

Faria gave a bitter laugh. 'Oh, my poor young fool!' he cried. 'Did Villefort make you promise never to speak the name of Noirtier?'

Dantès nodded.

'Noirtier is Villefort's father!' Faria said. 'He burned that letter to protect his career. His father is a Bonapartist, and this letter would have damaged Villefort's political progress. He sent you here to be sure of your silence.'

Dantès gave a cry. He returned to his dungeon and lay on his bed for hours, in silent meditation.

Now he thought of only one thing: revenge.

***

Dantès and Faria dug for 15 months to complete their tunnel. As they worked, Faria taught the young man everything he knew: history, physics, languages, mathematics and much more. One day, Faria told Dantès about an enormous fortune he had inherited, which lay buried on the deserted island of Monte Cristo.

'I am not mad, Edmond,' he insisted. 'My treasure *does* exist. And if I die before I escape, you shall have it.'

One night, Edmond heard a cry. When he reached Faria's cell, he saw that his friend was close to death.

'Do not forget Monte Cristo!' Faria cried, falling back on his bed. 'If you manage to escape, enjoy my treasure, for you have suffered enough.'

As day broke, Dantès saw that his friend was dead.

'I don't want to die in prison!' he thought. 'I want to punish my enemies. But only the dead leave this place…Ah...!'

And that was how the idea came to Dantès: to change places with his dear old friend in the burial sack, which would be tossed into the sea. Soon Dantès felt himself flying through the air. Then he plunged like an arrow into icy water. He quickly cut open the sack and the rope that tied him to a cannonball, and rose to the surface.

After 14 years of captivity, Dantès was free.

It was many months before Dantès reached the island of Monte Cristo, which lay between the islands of Elba and Corsica. Father Faria was right. Hidden deep in the caves, he found more treasure than he could have imagined. Returning to his home in Marseilles, he discovered that his father had died. Disguised as a priest called Father Busoni, he went to visit his old friend, Caderousse, who now ran an inn on the Bellegarde Road in Beaucaire.

'I have come from the death bed of poor Edmond

Dantès, who has died in prison,' he said. 'He begged me to clear his name and to give this to his dear friends.' Father Busoni took a beautiful diamond from his pocket. 'A friend, an ex-prisoner, left him this when he died. Tell me, Caderousse, do you know why Dantès was imprisoned? Do you know his friends?'

'Yes,' Caderousse replied, 'and I'll tell you everything if you promise not to repeat a word, for Edmond's friends are now important people.'

And in this way, Dantès learned of the letter that Danglars had written; that Danglars was now a rich man because he had made a fortune supplying the French army during the war in Spain, and because of his marriage to a banker's daughter; that Fernand, the poorest of them all, had joined the army and been awarded his title of count, as well as medals for services to his country; and that Mercédès had finally married him. They had a son called Albert. To his sorrow, he learned that Monsieur Morrel was on the brink of ruin because his ship was lost at sea.

Giving the diamond to Caderousse, Dantès went at once to Monsieur Morrel's house and, in secret, left money for his dear friend, saving his life and his reputation.

'Now I'm free to plot my revenge,' he said to himself. 'Danglars, Caderousse, Fernand – and, above all, Monsieur de Villefort.'

CHAPTER THREE

The Island of Monte Cristo

At the beginning of 1838, two young French noblemen planned to meet in Rome for the carnival: Franz d'Epinay and the Viscount Albert de Morcerf. Before Albert arrived, Franz decided to visit Elba. On the return journey, the boatman said there was good hunting on a nearby island.

'It's called Monte Cristo, sir,' he said. 'It's deserted, except for smugglers who sometimes shelter there.'

When they reached the shore, Franz was worried. There were men on the island. But they invited Franz to dine in a luxurious cave. His host was a pale man, in oriental clothing, who gave his name as 'Sinbad the Sailor', because he had travelled a great deal.

'Have you suffered, Monsieur?' Franz asked. 'You have the look of a man who has been persecuted by society.'

'No! I am the happiest man I know!' he replied. 'I am as free as a bird. I can go anywhere I choose.'

After he had eaten and drunk well, Franz fell asleep. When he awoke back on the hillside, he wondered if it had all been a dream. But when he returned to the others, he saw a small boat out to sea and, through his spyglass, he saw 'Sinbad the Sailor' waving farewell to him.

***

When Albert de Morcerf arrived in Rome, the two young men decided to visit the ruins of the Coliseum by night. But the innkeeper warned them to take care: the bandit

Luigi Vampa often ambushed travellers in the dark. Leaving Albert with a guide, Franz sat in the shadows of the Coliseum to wait. Here, he overheard a conversation, and was certain that one of the voices belonged to 'Sinbad the Sailor'. He did not sleep well that night, for the thought of that stranger haunted him. The next evening, at the opera, he saw the man again.

Another surprise awaited Franz. When he returned to his hotel, he was told that one of the guests – the Count of Monte Cristo – would like to be introduced to them both. As the door opened, Franz remained rooted to the spot. The man who came towards them was the cloaked figure at the Coliseum, the stranger in the box at the opera – and his host on the island of Monte Cristo.

On the last night of the carnival, as the candles went out, Albert felt himself being dragged into a carriage. Several hours later, Franz received a ransom note: Albert was being held by the bandit, Luigi Vampa. Thanks to the Count of Monte Cristo, Albert was released without payment. But the count shuddered as Albert shook his hand.

'What is wrong, Franz?' Albert asked his friend the next morning. 'I must admit that the count is an odd man, but you seem very cold towards him.'

Swearing Albert to secrecy, Franz told him about his visit to the island of Monte Cristo. 'How does Monte Cristo come to know Luigi Vampa so well?' he asked.

'The count is a rich traveller, that is all,' Albert replied. 'He bought an island and took its name. And those smugglers in his crew are not thieves, but exiles from their own land. Monte Cristo saved my life, and I shall do all I can for him when he visits Paris in May.'

CHAPTER FOUR

House of Secrets

Three months later, in Paris, Albert de Morcerf was preparing to receive the Count of Monte Cristo. Several guests had been invited to meet him, including Maximilien Morrel, the son of the ship owner who had died some years before. During the conversation, Albert talked of his forthcoming engagement to Eugénie Danglars.

'Eugénie Danglars!' Monte Cristo exclaimed. 'Isn't her father now Baron Danglars?'

'Yes,' Albert replied.

When the others had left, Albert showed the count around his apartment. In the bedroom, Monte Cristo went straight to a portrait on the wall. It showed a young woman of about 25, wearing a red and black bodice, her dark hair held back by gold pins. She was staring sadly at the sea.

The count's cheeks paled.

'This is my mother,' Albert said. 'She had this painting done some years ago, dressed in that fisherwoman's costume. My father does not like it. So I keep it here. My mother cannot look at it without weeping.'

Albert's father – the Count de Morcerf – welcomed Monte Cristo warmly. But when his wife appeared in the doorway, she turned deadly pale. 'I owe you my son's life, sir,' she said, staring at him, 'and I bless you for that.'

Monte Cristo bowed, his face even paler than hers.

Later, when he had gone, the countess asked her son, 'What is this title of Monte Cristo?'

'It is a place, Mother,' he replied. 'The count bought an

island in the Mediterranean Sea, the haunt of smugglers. He is not a nobleman, but his manners are better than many noblemen I have met. Yes, he is a remarkable man.'

'Do you like him?' his mother asked.

'Yes, even though Franz dislikes him,' Albert said. 'He thinks that Monte Cristo is a ghost returned from the dead.'

His mother shrank back in terror. 'Take care, Albert,' she whispered.

***

Monte Cristo had bought a house in Auteuil, on the outskirts of Paris. As he and his servant, Bertuccio, approached it, his servant became more and more nervous. Night had fallen and the house had a gloomy air.

'What was the name of the man who owned this house?' Monte Cristo asked the caretaker.

'The Marquis de Saint-Méran,' the man replied. 'He had an only daughter, whom he married to Monsieur de Villefort, the king's prosecutor.'

Bertuccio was paler than the wall against which he was leaning. After looking around the house, the count asked to see the garden.

'No, no!' Bertuccio cried. 'I can't go there! If only you'd told me *this* was the house you'd bought. It's the house of murder! It was an act of revenge. *He* fell just there, beside the hole where he'd buried his child…'

'Who?' the count asked.

'Monsieur de Villefort!'

'Impossible!' the count replied. 'Well, Bertuccio, you must tell me what happened.'

'It all goes back to 1815,' Bertuccio began. 'My brother was murdered and I went to Villefort to ask him to investigate the crime. But he refused, because my brother supported Napoleon. I threatened to kill him. When he moved to Paris, I followed him. I often saw him walking in the garden of this house with a pregnant woman. One night, I took out my dagger and waited. As midnight struck, Villefort came from the house alone. But he began to dig a hole, in which he placed a small box. I leapt at him, stabbing him and shouting my name. He fell at once. I grabbed the box and ran. Inside…was a baby. I breathed air into his lungs and life came back to him. My brother's wife decided to take him in. She brought him up, although he grew into a wicked child. We named him Benedetto.'

'You should have returned the child to its mother, Bertuccio,' the count replied. 'That was your true crime.'

'I'd gone back to smuggling after my brother's death,' Bertuccio continued, 'and I planned to ask a sea captain to take the boy on. One night, I went to my usual inn, run by a man called Caderousse…'

'When was that?'

'June, 1829. But Caderousse had a visitor, a jeweller who'd come to buy a diamond that a priest called Father Busoni had given him. Well, in short, Caderousse murdered his wife and the jeweller and made off with the money and the diamond. The police found me hiding there and blamed me for the murder. You know the rest. Father Busoni rescued me from prison and found me work with you.'

'What happened to Benedetto?' Monte Cristo asked.

'He ended up in prison,' Bertuccio shuddered. 'He stole from my sister-in-law and set fire to her house. I hope he's dead! And I still do not know if Villefort died at my feet.'

'Anything is possible,' the count muttered.

CHAPTER FIVE

The Trap Tightens

The Count of Monte Cristo was visiting Baron Danglars at his mansion. A look of disgust passed over his face.

'He looks like a snake and a vulture at the same time,' he thought.

Danglars took a letter from his pocket. 'I have a letter to my bank asking me to lend you as much money as you need while you are in France,' he said. 'I do not understand, Monsieur.'

'Why not?' the count asked. '*My* bank lends me as much money as I need. Why does your bank not do the same?'

'Do not worry, Monsieur, we shall meet your needs…' Danglars wiped the sweat from his forehead. 'Even if you were to ask for a million francs…'

'What use would a million be to me?' the count asked, taking a million francs in bonds from his pocket. Danglars reeled with shock. 'I shall need to borrow six million francs a year,' he finished.

'Very well!' Danglars replied, choking. 'Now you must meet my wife.'

And it was the Baroness Danglars who told Monte Cristo that her friend - Madame de Villefort – had asked to borrow her young and frisky horses for a carriage ride to Auteuil the very next day. That evening, Monte Cristo left for Auteuil.

***

The next afternoon, the count summoned his servant, Ali.

'I hear that you are skilled with the lasso,' the count said. 'Could you stop two horses in their tracks – right outside my house? They will be pulling a carriage.'

Ali nodded.

At five o'clock, the sound of horses' hooves thundered in the distance. The horses were out of control. Inside the carriage, a woman clutched her young son to her in terror. As soon as the horses approached the count's house, Ali took a lasso from his pocket and threw it around one of the horses' legs, bringing it to the ground. Monte Cristo rushed to the carriage and took the mother and child inside.

'I am Madame Héloïse de Villefort,' the woman whispered. 'And this is my son, Edouard. How can I thank you for saving us?'

The incident became the talk of Paris that evening. Monsieur de Villefort got into his coach and set off for the count's house. He had married again after the death of his first wife, and had a daughter, Valentine, from his first marriage, as well as little Edouard. To his friends, he was a powerful protector. To his enemies, he was silent and without feeling. This was the same man whom Edmond Dantès had faced in Marseilles in 1815, although his pale skin was now yellow, his eyes sunken. He was dressed in black, except for a red ribbon in his buttonhole, like a line of blood.

Monte Cristo greeted him with an icy coldness. After receiving Villefort's thanks, they talked about justice and the law.

'So you believe that human nature is weak,' Villefort said, 'and that *every* man has committed some error?'

'Some error…or crime,' the count replied.

Villefort turned the talk to his father, Monsieur Noirtier

de Villefort, who was now paralysed after a stroke.

'I believe he was struck down by God for his sins,' Villefort said.

Monte Cristo had a smile on his lips, but he gave a

silent scream that would have put Villefort to flight if he
had heard it.

'Yes, Villefort still lives!' he thought. 'And my heart is
still full of poison.'

CHAPTER SIX

Money, Love and Hate

In the beautiful garden of Monsieur de Villefort's house, Valentine Villefort was in secret conversation with Maximilien Morrel. The two young people were very much in love – in spite of the fact that Villefort was planning to marry her to Franz d'Epinay.

'Valentine, I have told nobody about my feelings for you,' Morrel said. 'But I long to tell that extraordinary man I met last week at Albert's. You know him, too. He saved your stepmother's life.'

'The Count of Monte Cristo?' she cried, shuddering. 'No! A friend of *hers* cannot be a friend of mine!'

'But he also rescued Albert de Morcerf from the bandits,' Morrel replied. 'He obviously has the power to influence what will happen.'

'What has he done for you?' Valentine asked.

'Nothing I know of,' Morrel replied. 'But, like the sun, he warms me just by being there.'

***

As this conversation was taking place, Villefort had gone to talk to his father about Valentine's marriage. Noirtier was violently opposed to it. When Valentine came to join them, she embraced the old man.

'I, too, am very unhappy about this marriage, Grandfather,' she said. 'I do not love Franz d'Epinay.'

Noirtier's eyes filled with tears. He indicated that a

solicitor should be brought to the house so that he could change his will. If Valentine married Franz, she would inherit nothing of his great fortune.

Villefort was the first to break the astonished silence at the news. 'I am the master of my daughter,' he said. 'I want her to marry Franz d'Epinay. So she *will* marry him. I do not care about your will, Father.'

Valentine fell into a chair, weeping.

***

An unfashionable man of about 52, a Major Cavalcanti, arrived at Monte Cristo's house in Paris. He had been summoned there by a letter from Father Busoni, telling him that Monte Cristo had found his son, Andrea. The poor child had been kidnapped at the age of five – 15 years earlier. The count greeted him warmly, gave him money and new clothes – and the baptismal certificate of his son.

Andrea Cavalcanti, who had also been summoned by a letter, this time from 'Sinbad the Sailor', was a tall, young man with blond hair and a reddish beard, and dark eyes. He was very ready to take up the large fortune the count had promised him, on condition that Andrea stayed in Paris.

"Sinbad the Sailor' is an eccentric English friend of mine called Lord Wilmore,' Monte Cristo explained.

Monte Cristo left the father and son alone.

'Do you understand what is going on?' Old Cavalcanti asked in Italian.

'Good heavens, no!' Andrea replied.

'All this has been planned to fool someone,' the old man said.

'But not you or me, so why worry?' Andrea replied.

***

The next morning, Monte Cristo rode out of Paris to a telegraph station used for sending messages. There, with bundles of bank notes, he bribed the telegraph man to send an incorrect message to the French government: that the king of Spain had escaped from his exile and that a rebellion was about to break out in Spain. When Danglars heard of this from a friend, he quickly sold the shares he held in the Spanish government.

But the very next day, the report was said to be false. Poor Danglars! As the share prices rose, he lost about a million francs by selling his shares when he need not have done.

Once more, Monte Cristo smiled with quiet satisfaction.

CHAPTER SEVEN

Ghosts from the Past

The gloomy house in Auteuil, which had been empty for 25 years, had come to life, because Monte Cristo was giving a party for his new friends.

When Danglars arrived, the baron's face was pale, as if he had just stepped from his tomb. When Villefort arrived, Monte Cristo felt his hand tremble in their handshake.

Bertuccio appeared in the doorway to count the guests for dinner. 'Oh, my God!' he whispered to his master. 'The Baroness Danglars! That's *her*, the woman who was pregnant.' Then he saw Villefort. 'So I didn't kill him!'

'No, your dagger must have missed his heart,' the count replied. 'Do not forget that young man in the black coat. He is Monsieur Andrea Cavalcanti.'

'Benedetto!' Bertuccio whispered.

And Monte Cristo silenced him with a cold look.

After the meal, which was magnificent, the count showed the guests around his house.

'There is a room upstairs which is very sinister,' he said. 'Come, let me show you.'

This room was unlit and hung with blood-red tapestries. Villefort's face was ashen. Madame Danglars slumped into a chair.

'And there is a small staircase leading to the garden,' Monte Cristo said. 'You can imagine a crime being committed here.'

Madame Danglars almost fainted at his words. Villefort leaned against a wall.

'You're terrifying the ladies, Count!' he cried.

'Good Lord!' Monte Cristo said. 'Then let us imagine this room to be that of a respectable mother of a family…'

At his words, Madame Danglars fainted away. When she had recovered, Monte Cristo took her arm and led her down to the garden. 'There really was a crime committed here,' he said, taking Villefort's arm, too. 'Here, in this very spot, while my men were digging, they found the skeleton of a newborn child.'

'Who says it was a crime?' Villefort asked, his voice trembling.

Seeing that his guests could bear no more, Monte Cristo had coffee served. And shortly afterwards, they left for home.

As Andrea Cavalcanti climbed into his carriage, a hand touched his shoulder. He half turned and saw a man with a mocking smile, who called him Benedetto and got into the carriage beside him.

'Take care, Caderousse,' Andrea said. 'Monte Cristo has found my father.'

'Your *real* father?'

'No, but I do not care,' the young man laughed. 'As long as he gives me what I want.'

'And as long as you give me what I want,' Caderousse replied. 'Let's say, two hundred francs a month to keep me quiet, eh?'

'Alas!' Andrea said, with a sigh. 'One can never be completely happy in this world.'

***

The next day, after a sleepless night, Baroness Danglars made her way to Villefort's office.

'You will agree that if I did make a mistake, I was severely punished for it last night,' she wept.

'You must be brave, Madame!' Villefort replied. 'It is not ended yet! You only see the past. But the future may be terrible, and stained with blood.'

Madame Danglars stifled a cry.

'How has this terrible past been brought alive?' Villefort asked. 'Not by chance. Listen, I must tell you what I could not tell you all those years ago! Many months later, when I had recovered from my wounds – when I discovered that you had married Danglars – I went back to the garden at Auteuil. I found nothing. *Nothing*! The box had vanished!'

'*Vanished?*' Madame Danglars could hardly speak in her horror. 'Oh, my poor child!'

'Do you understand now?' Villefort asked. 'The child must be alive. Somebody shares our secret. And if Monte Cristo knows the spot, then *he* knows our secret.' He looked at Madame Danglars. 'I warn you against *him*,' he whispered. 'By the end of this week, I shall find out who Monte Cristo is, where he comes from, where he is going to – and why he tells us about a child dug up in his garden.'

Villefort spoke these words in a tone of voice that would have made Monte Cristo shudder if he had heard them.

CHAPTER EIGHT

Meetings in the Dark

After the dinner at Monte Cristo's house, Madame Danglars could not think of the count without trembling. And Villefort could find out very little about him, except that Father Busoni and Lord Wilmore were his close friends. But neither of the men, who both happened to be in Paris, could tell him anything more.

The hot days of July brought an important social event: the ball of Albert de Morcerf. When Monte Cristo came in, everybody stared. It was not just his black coat and white waistcoat which attracted attention, but his face, calm and innocent, his curly black hair, his sad eyes, and most of all, his mouth, which could so easily show contempt.

Albert's mother could not take her eyes off him. At last, she asked him to walk with her in the garden. Monte Cristo seemed to stagger for a moment. Outside, she clasped his arm with both hands. The count turned as pale as death.

'Monsieur,' the countess said, 'is it true that you have seen much, travelled far and suffered deeply?'

'Yes. I loved a girl and was going to marry her,' the count replied, 'but…the war came and swept me from her world…When I came back, she was married.'

'Yes,' she whispered, 'we only love once in our life! Did you ever see her again?'

'Never,' he replied.

'And have you forgiven her?' Mercédès asked.

'I think so,' he replied. 'But *only* her. Not those who separated us.'

Valentine was called away from the ball by the news of the death of the Marquis de Saint-Méran, her maternal grandfather. His death was swiftly followed by the death of his wife. The doctor confided his terrible thoughts to Villefort: that both of them had been poisoned.

As soon as the burials had taken place, Villefort arranged for the marriage contract to be signed. Whilst the lawyer set out the papers, Noirtier asked to see Franz.

'Here he is, Father,' Villefort said. 'I am sure that your opposition to this marriage will disappear once you have spoken to him.'

Noirtier gave a look that turned Villefort's blood to ice. Letters were taken from a secret drawer and given to Franz to read. They told him about his father's death. He was killed in a duel when Franz was only two years old, because he supported the king of France, not Napoleon.

'In heaven's name, sir!' Franz begged Noirtier. 'Tell me the name of the man who killed my poor father!'

'It was *me*,' Noirtier indicated.

Franz slumped into a chair. And hours later, he withdrew from his engagement to Valentine. Old Noirtier changed his will once more to allow Valentine to inherit his fortune. He also planned to leave Villefort's house. Valentine would live with him until she was 21, when she would marry Morrel. Now happiness was in their grasp at last.

***

The marriage arrangements between Eugénie Danglars and Albert de Morcerf were also progressing badly. Baron Danglars had withdrawn his consent because of a newspaper article which tarnished the reputation of Albert's father, Fernand. Albert was led to believe that Monte Cristo was responsible.

At once, Andrea Cavalcanti declared his interest in marrying Eugénie. When he went to give Caderousse his money, his friend laughed.

'Huh! So you're marrying the daughter of my old friend, Danglars!' he cried. 'I need more money, Benedetto! Tell me the layout of your count's house and I'll pay him a surprise visit in the dark.'

That night, Monte Cristo watched a man enter his house through an upstairs window. But, as a ray of light shone across the thief's face, he whispered in surprise, 'Well, it's my old friend!' At once, he changed into priest's clothes, putting on a metal chain vest under his robe. Then he took a candle and opened the door.

'Good evening, dear Monsieur Caderousse,' he said. 'What the devil are you doing here at this hour, my fine murderer?'

'Father Busoni!' Caderousse cried, staring in horror. 'It must be almost ten years since you brought me that diamond!' He came closer. 'I won't go back to prison!' he cried, striking the priest's chest with his dagger. But it fell to the ground.

The count gripped Caderousse's arm. 'Now write down exactly what I say!' he ordered. With a trembling hand, Caderousse wrote the following:

"To Baron Danglars: The man to whom you are to marry your daughter – Andrea Cavalcanti – is an escaped prisoner called Benedetto."

Monte Cristo took the letter and let Caderousse escape. But as Caderousse climbed over the wall, a man came from the shadows and stabbed him. With his dying breath, Caderousse told the priest that Benedetto had murdered him, and signed a note to that effect. The count held up his candle.

'Look carefully, Caderousse,' he whispered. He took off his wig and let down his long black hair. 'Go back to your earliest memories.'

'Yes,' Caderousse gasped. 'I did know you once…who are you?'

The count bent over the dying man and whispered in his ear, 'Edmond Dantès!'

'Oh, my God, forgive me!' Caderousse cried.

And when the doctor and Villefort arrived, they found Father Busoni praying over the dead man.

***

Albert de Morcerf confronted Monte Cristo at the opera. White and trembling, he rushed into the count's box, where the count was sitting with Morrel.

'I have come for an explanation, sir,' he cried. 'Why have you insulted my father so publicly?'

'I do not know what you mean,' the count replied.

Albert took off his glove and would have thrown it at the count's feet, to challenge him to a duel, if Morrel had not grabbed his wrist.

'Monsieur Albert,' Monte Cristo said, in a terrifying voice. 'I shall send your glove back to you wrapped around a bullet. By tomorrow morning, I shall have killed you.'

CHAPTER NINE

A Mother's Love

As Monte Cristo was preparing his pistols that night, a veiled woman was shown into his room.

'It is not Madame de Morcerf who has come to you, Edmond,' she whispered. 'It is Mercédès.'

'Mercédès is dead to me, Madame,' he replied.

'Mercédès is alive,' she insisted. 'And she recognised your voice as soon as she heard it. I knew it was you who had insulted Monsieur de Morcerf.'

'Fernand, you mean, Madame,' the count said, full of hatred.

'If you want to take your revenge, take it on me, Edmond,' she replied. 'I do not know why you were arrested on our wedding day.'

Monte Cristo handed Mercédès the letter that Danglars had written that February day. 'It cost me a great deal of money,' he said, 'but it is worth it to prove to you that I am taking my revenge on Fernand the fisherman, not on Fernand the general.'

When Mercédès had read the letter, she fell to her knees. 'Forgive me!' she cried. 'I still love you, Edmond.'

'I *must* have my revenge!' Monte Cristo cried.

A shudder of fear ran through Mercédès' body. 'But not on my son, Edmond! Spare him!' she begged.

'Fernand's son insulted me in public,' Monte Cristo replied, 'and the duel *will* take place.' He looked at Mercédès and sighed. 'But I shall let your son kill me, Madame, for your sake.'

'Thank you!' she cried. 'Goodbye, Edmond.'

The count gave a bitter smile. *How quickly she accepted,* he thought. *She cares more for her son than she does for me. I shall not regret my death, but I regret that my revenge, so carefully plotted through these long years, will be destroyed, all because my heart still feels love for Mercédès.*

***

Albert was late for the duel. He was pale and had not slept all night.

'Monsieur,' he said in an unsteady voice. 'You were right to take your revenge on my father, now that my mother has told me what he did to you so many years ago.'

It was like a thunderbolt. Monte Cristo stared at him in astonishment. Then, with tears in his eyes, he shook Albert's hand.

Mercédès has saved my life by confessing that terrible family secret, he thought. *What courage she has!*

But Monte Cristo's troubles were not finished. Albert's father came straight to his house, declaring his desire to fight in place of his son.

'I do not know you, but I hate you!' Fernand de Morcerf cried. 'I want to know your true name before I plunge my sword into your heart!'

Monte Cristo's eyes burned with anger. He rushed from the room and came back wearing a sailor's uniform like the one he had worn on board his ship.

'Fernand!' he cried. 'You can guess my name, can't you? Look at my face, now that it is lit up by the joy of revenge. You must have seen it often in your dreams since your marriage to my fiancée, Mercédès.'

The general, with a look of horror, cried, 'Edmond Dantès!'

He dragged himself out to his carriage. And, as soon as he reached home, he shot himself.

***

Meanwhile, in the Villefort household, Valentine was taken ill with suspected poisoning with the same medicine her grandfather took. Only then did Morrel reveal to Monte Cristo how much he loved her. Only then did Old Noirtier indicate that he had long feared this and had, for many weeks, given his granddaughter some of his own medicine to drink. In this way, he protected her against a possible overdose. Thanks to her grandfather, Valentine did not die, although she remained very ill.

One night she saw Monte Cristo leaning over her bed.

'Do not be afraid,' he whispered. 'I am watching over you for Maximilien, and I have seen who has been poisoning you every night. I have poured away that poison. Pretend to be asleep and you will see, too!'

Valentine did as the count asked. And, after midnight, she saw her stepmother pouring out her nightly poison and creeping from her bedroom.

'Let me escape from this house!' she wept, when the count returned.

'She will follow you wherever you go, Valentine,' Monte Cristo replied. 'She wants your fortune for her son. Now you must do what I ask if you wish to live.'

'Monsieur, I love Maximilien and therefore I will do anything to stay alive,' she replied.

'Then swallow this tablet,' he whispered, 'and fear nothing. I shall be watching over you.'

***

The marriage contract between Eugénie Danglars and Andrea Cavalcanti was to be signed at nine o'clock in the evening. As guests gathered for the occasion, talk turned to the murder at Monte Cristo's house.

'In fact, the police found a letter on the murdered man, addressed to you, Baron,' the count said. Andrea's face turned pale. 'The murdered man was called Caderousse.'

When Danglars called for Andrea to sign the contract, he had already slipped from the room. Soon afterwards, two policemen entered, demanding to see him.

'But why do you want *him?*' Danglars asked.

'He's an ex-convict who's murdered Caderousse,' one of the policemen explained. 'They were in prison together.'

After this shocking news, Eugénie Danglars ran away in the middle of the night.

'Fortunately you are rich, Baron Danglars,' Monte Cristo said, 'and your fortune does not depend upon your daughter's marriage.'

'Ah, yes, I am still rich!' the baron boasted. 'In fact, I am about to take out five million francs in cash from my bank to settle some urgent debts. Can you believe it?'

'Well, I can test it for myself,' Monte Cristo replied, smiling. 'You remember I have a credit limit of six million francs with you. Well, I have already borrowed almost a million. But I am in great need of money at the moment. Let me have the other five million today.'

Danglars was stricken with terror. He laughed nervously.

'My bank does not have ten million francs!' he thought. 'Now I face ruin.'

Tragedy had befallen both the Danglars and the Villeforts, but the Villefort tragedy was greater, for Valentine was suddenly found dead. At her burial in the family tomb, Morrel was pale and silent, since only Monte Cristo knew his secret love for her. The count hurried from the burial to Morrel's house. He found him planning to kill himself.

'*I* will prevent you!' Monte Cristo said.

'Who are you, to think you have such power?' Morrel asked.

'*Who* am I?' the count asked. 'I am the *only* man who can say, 'I do not want your father's son to die today.'

'Why do you mention my father?'

'I was the man who saved his life, ten years ago today, on the fifth of September,' Monte Cristo replied. 'He was going to kill himself because he had lost all his money. Maximilien, *I* was the man who sent money to him, although he did not know it had come from me. I am Edmond Dantès.'

Morrel shrank back, astonished. 'Have no fear, sir,' he whispered. 'I shall no longer look for death, but my grief will kill me anyway.'

'You will thank me one day for saving your life,' the count said. 'But if, in a month from today, I have not cured you of your grief, I shall give you the same poison that killed Valentine.'

CHAPTER TEN

Too Much Revenge

On a splendid autumn day, Andrea Cavalcanti, also known as Benedetto, was brought to trial in Paris. Villefort was the chief prosecutor. Before he left for court, he demanded to speak to his wife. 'Where do you keep the poison that has killed my father-in-law, my mother-in-law and my daughter?' he asked. She shrank back from him. 'So you do not deny it?' he cried. 'I repeat, where is *your* poison?'

'Oh, sir, you cannot want me to kill myself!' his wife wept.

'I do not want you to be executed in public,' he replied. 'I am on my way to court to try one murderer. If you are not dead by the time I come back, I shall have you arrested.'

Villefort was as pale as death when Benedetto was brought into court.

'Where were you born?' the judge asked the accused.

'Auteuil, near Paris,' Benedetto replied.

'What is your name?'

'I cannot tell it,' the accused replied, 'but I know my father's name.' He paused. 'It is Monsieur de Villefort.'

A cry rose from the crowd like a peal of thunder.

'My father told my mother that I was dead,' he went on, 'and he buried me alive in the garden. Somebody saw him. That is how I know. I do not know my mother's name, but she has done nothing wrong.'

Madame Danglars fell to the ground, screaming.

'Everything this young man has said is true,' Villefort

whispered, rising to his feet. His teeth chattered like a man with a fever as he staggered towards the door. Everybody was speechless. It was a terrible end to all the events that had shaken Parisian society for more than two weeks.

At his house, Villefort broke open the door of the bedroom where his wife fell dying at his feet. In the next room, he found the body of his young son. He staggered on to his father's rooms, his hair standing on end with shock. There he found him with Father Busoni.

'So *you* are here, Monsieur!' Villefort cried. 'Do you always appear when there is death in my house?'

'I have come to tell you that you have paid your debt to me,' the priest said.

'My God!' Villefort cried. 'That is not the voice of Father Busoni!' As he watched, Busoni tore off his wig and shook his black hair over his shoulders. 'That is the face of Monte Cristo!'

'Think further back, Villefort!' the count said.

'You are *not* Busoni! You are *not* Monte Cristo!' Villefort muttered.

'You condemned me to a slow and terrible death,' Monte Cristo whispered. 'You deprived me of love, as well as my freedom. I am the ghost of that man you locked up almost 24 years ago.'

'You are…' Villefort began. 'Edmond Dantès!' Villefort cried, dragging him towards his apartment. 'Then look, Edmond Dantès! Look at the bodies of my wife and child! Now you have your revenge.'

Monte Cristo turned pale. *That poor child!* he thought. *I have taken my revenge too far.*

On arriving home, the count sent for Morrel. 'Get ready, Maximilien,' he said. 'We shall leave Paris tomorrow.'

'Have you nothing more to do here?' Morrel asked.

'No,' Monte Cristo replied. 'I have done too much already. Now I have plans to carry out elsewhere. Meet me on the island of Monte Cristo on the fifth day of October, Maximilien. There I shall keep my promise to you. If you still grieve for Valentine, I shall give you poison.'

***

Baron Danglars, escaping his ruin in Paris, had reached Italy, where he planned to live on the money he had taken with him. But, outside Rome, he was kidnapped by Luigi Vampa and paid so dearly for his food while in captivity that his money ran out.

'Do you repent for the evil you have done?' a voice asked. Danglars saw a cloaked man standing in the shadows of the cave in which he was held.

'Yes,' Danglars whispered in terror.

'Then I pardon you!' the man said. He stepped forward and threw off his cloak.

'The Count of Monte Cristo!' Danglars cried.

'I am not the Count of Monte Cristo. I am the man you betrayed all those years ago. I am Edmond Dantès!'

Danglars gave a cry and fell to the ground. And when he looked up, he saw only a shadow disappearing from his sight.

***

Monte Cristo returned to his father's house in Marseilles. At the count's request, Mercédès was living there alone, for Albert had joined the army.

'I was the guilty one, Edmond,' Mercédès wept. 'The others acted out of greed, hatred and selfishness. But I was a coward. I should not have married Fernand.' She touched his hand, and looked to the sky. 'Farewell, dear Edmond. Let us hope we meet after death,' she said.

Monte Cristo went from Mercédès to the Château d'If, as he had done so many years before on that February night. It was no longer a prison. Only a caretaker remained there. The count went to see his old cell, and the tunnel he had dug to reach Father Faria.

'Are there any interesting tales told of this awful place?' he asked.

'Oh, yes!' the caretaker replied. 'In 1829, a prisoner escaped by hiding in a burial sack. The guards heard a terrible cry as it hit the water. Poor man, he would have drowned.'

'Did they know his name?' the count asked.

'Number 34,' the caretaker replied.

On the fifth of October, a yacht brought Maximilien Morrel to the island of Monte Cristo. The count was waiting to greet him, and he saw that the young man was still pale with grief.

Monte Cristo kept his promise. At midnight, Morrel swallowed the potion to end his grief. But, to his surprise, he awoke the next morning to find Valentine by his side.

'The Count of Monte Cristo saved me, too,' she whispered. 'He gave me a potion to make me appear dead.'

As they stood looking out to sea, they saw a white sail on the horizon.

'Monte Cristo has gone!' Morrel cried. 'Farewell, my friend! Will we ever meet again?'

'My dearest,' Valentine said. 'The count has taught us one thing, that we must remember these two words: wait and hope.'